SALAD DAYS

maudlinhouse.net
twitter.com/maudlinhouse

SALAD DAYS
Copyright © 2021 by Laura Theobald

Cover artwork: Gabby Oh
Cover design: Laura Theobald

PRAISE FOR *SALAD DAYS*

"This is my favorite kind of poetry: dry, real, hilarious, sharp, surreal, poignant, unapologetically itself. Laura's singular charmingly unmoored voice offers surprise after surprise in this collection. I started copying and pasting my favorite lines into an email draft, which quickly turned into copying and pasting entire poems, before I realized I'd soon have an email draft containing an exact copy of the book. *Salad Days* is 'a planet nobody asked for'–like how the best gifts aren't requestable–a life-giving planet for self-conscious folks with thirsty imaginations, accessible only by reading. It's a love letter to the future–not the kind of love letter that gushes with promises and pathos, the kind that arrives after truly knowing the faulted gritty humanity of another with whom you can be nothing but honest. If you lurk on social media and silently lament, 'where did all the interesting stuff go, isn't anyone doing anything new anymore,' this is the book for you."

– Megan Boyle, author of *Liveblog* and *Selected Unpublished Blog Posts of a Mexican Panda Express Employee*

"I don't usually like poetry. 98% of poetry is overwrought and academic and boring. But Laura Theobald is mad (like Sylvia Plath mad, not the other kind) which makes her poetry different, in the way a mad woman's voice is always a little different. In a way I like. In a way that intrigues me. Listen to her."

– Elizabeth Ellen, author of *Person/a* and *Her Lesser Work*

"Are you sure you can call it poetry if it is this fun and cool? This is a stunning collection that gives equal respect and curiosity to the simple and profound dramas of human life. I felt very uplifted reading it. Several times I thought, 'I should get this poem tattooed on me' and I do not normally think things like that. I think I just wanted ownership of the poems. *Salad Days* gives attention to the quiet moments and the cartoonish ones, and the people we lust over and the people who are ruining the world. It is delicate and unflinching and effortless and fun and so, so important."

– Chelsea Martin, author of *Caca Dolce* and *Even Though I Don't Miss You*

"Laura Theobald is a powerful artist, fully expressed. Joy, anger, soaring highs balanced against crushing lows—all of it lives boldly in her work. I enjoyed *Salad Days* immensely."

– Bud Smith

"I've long been in awe of Laura Theobald's poetry: few other poets are able to make the mundane feel grandiose & eventful with such an eloquent & hilarious tenderness. *Salad Days* is no different: the poems in this collection are short and opulent and in love, but they are also out of love and out of patience. Though there is longing & sadness here, it exists alongside an effusive & effortless joy for the inevitable truths that failure & disappointment reveal. It's this synthesis that makes this book special. 'I was put on this earth to entertain myself / and I am killing it,' says Theobald, and *Salad Days* is killing it, too."

– Mark Cugini, author of *I Am Going to Steal the Declaration of Independence* and *Poetry Magazine*

"*Salad Days* simplifies the confusion of caring for someone else by comparing our relationships to those we have with the lifeless objects that make up our lives. Environments become museum of our emotions. Laura Theobald guides us through with a sense of humor and safe- words. In this collection we see how "every single person is a self-contained universe" and in our own worlds we don't have to feel lonely. Objects are always around us even if no one is with us. "There is nirvana but there is no one to talk to" and in this space there's a sense of security, the kind that comes from the necessity to know one's self. Theobald shows how to find meaning in every little think, or put it there. By engaging with things as projections of feelings these poems evoke the complex emotions of being involved, what it really takes to feel alive."

– Catch Breath, author of *bleach tooth*

"The poems in Laura Theobald's *Salad Days* are funny, sweet, and restless. They'll call you a pussy and buy you a banana split. I love the fun Theobald makes of her world."

– Rachelle Toarmino, author of *That Ex*

"Laura Theobald's *Salad Days* speaks to everyone 'invested in a life of destruction.' At times a conversation and at others a secret rumination on purpose and desire that the reader feels privy to, Theobald's poetry sits at the intersection of lightness and heaviness—each poem building like the ticking of a time bomb. It is often the case that one must self-destruct in order to begin again; Laura's poetry asks what it means to be the 'bomb.'"

– Erin Taylor, author of *Bimboland* and Arts Editor at *Observer*

"Something about *Salad Days* reminds me of Emily Dickinson—if Emily were hornier and funnier. The poems have the kind of specificity that allows them to feel universal, like some beautiful, demented collective dream. Laura Theobald really is one of the best poets we have."

– Juliet Escoria, author of *Juliet the Maniac* and *Black Cloud*

"Swerving, honest, & exuberant, the poems in *Salad Days* document a continual knotting of simile & metaphor. The book's self in each poem is compared to some new thing, revealing the incessant reinterpretations & positionings that the lyric mind demands of a life. Laura Theobald makes poetry look easy, how a sudden slice across the finger while chopping onions makes blood look easy."

– Mathias Svalina, author of *The Depression*

SALAD
DAYS

Laura Theobald

My salad days,
When I was green in judgment, cold in blood.
To say as I said then! But come away;
Get me ink and paper.
He shall have every day a several greeting,
Or I'll unpeople Egypt.

- Antony and Cleopatra

WAVES OF CONFUSION

KITCHEN POEM

I was crooked before I met you
But now I am in dire straits
You act like everything is fine
I don't see why it should be like that
I think I'm missing a step
That is why I am not a social climber
Literally you mailed me an empty jar
Suddenly it is better not to be remembered
I'd like to go back to the kitchen now
I know it sounds bad but I can't help that

ANCESTOR POEM

My heart was calling out to you
But you were wearing headphones
It was like getting your period at a funeral
It was like being run over by a train-shaped cloud
What if I still felt like a person
Then I would not feel like a not-person
Then my sense of worth would no longer depend on
How much you like me at any given moment
It would be like solving a long equation
It would be like watching my ancestor fall off a roof

TOMATO POEM

Boy-child you drove a tricycle over me while pulling my hair
It was thoughtful kind of
But I was afraid that you were going to get hurt
I am totally confused
I can't wait to keep being exactly the same
It will be like having a circulatory system made out of lightning
And skin like a tomato
And sleeping on a trampoline every night

POTATO POEM

My best part of me comes out like a potato
And gets immediately lost
Anyway I'm glad you're not around anymore
I'm glad I'm a spectacular liar now
With these weird streaks under my eyes
I'm glad I spent all that time alone
I'm glad you said I appreciate you caring about me
I'm glad you are such a bitch
I bet you don't remember my face anymore
It happens fast
Like anything that is terrible

DIAMOND POEM

You are like a painting that has been painted over
With a less beautiful painting
I wanted to take you to an emergency shelter
I wanted to be at least as important as real estate
When I couldn't fix anything I just burned it down
Then I was just like everybody else
Then I did nothing
Then I was like nobody at all
It was like putting a bandage on a corpse
It was really unoriginal
It was my responsibility to make people care
But all I could think about was a diamond the size of a fist

ISLAND POEM

You cherished me
Like something that cannot yet be experienced online
I tried to stuff you entirely into my snatch like a stack of envelopes
I insisted on becoming very useless to myself
I built an island and watched you torch it
Like some kind of hideous adult
The only thing left is to never think of you again
Even as you are tossing me out of a boat
Sometimes you can know someone believes in you
When they are trying to kill you
In fact if I am not bludgeoned to death with a musical instrument
I will call you a pussy
If I am caught dead without gum in my hair
I will never say you are a true gangster
If you are looking for the bottom
It is probably already in you

ASS POEM

You have the finest ass I have ever touched
Great now I am full of despair
And I would like to be on fire
I am exactly like a Buddhist
Except my yoga instructor is always telling me
To stop congratulating myself
This is the only way I can reclaim my integrity!
I have to keep tearing you apart
All day I dream about sparagmos
I wonder what piece of you will end up in my mouth
I hope it is a good one

SHAKESPEARE POEM

What the fuck
I am exactly like Shakespeare
I was filling you up with hope
Like a balloon full of hope
It is impossible to be alive
I was put on this earth to entertain myself
And I am killing it
Also you are banished from this poem
The rest of this poem is about something else

PERENNIAL POEM

I am like a perennial
I am like a letter to myself always arriving
I am trying to love myself
And it is disgusting
It is like an advanced course in loneliness
I am listening to the sounds of the night
And I have to be listening to them
Unless I want to be listening to something else
I have arrived with feelings and a mouth
And now I have to be expanding sideways into myself
While the universe is crying quietly to itself and expanding

ONION POEM

What does it mean to wake up with an onion in your bed
I mean a whole literal onion
I am a terrible thief
I walk around putting onions in my purse
Taking advantage of how no one pays attention to me ever
I love it
I deserve it
I cried a little today
But my heart wasn't really in it
It was a little half-hearted cry
Should I fall in love yes or no
It is hard to decide
Seems like kind of a waste keeping it all to myself though
All of this onion action

FISH POEM

I am like this fish on the wall
Big glassy eyes looking
As long as you like
All I had to give was myself
And everything I had
And everything I might have had one day
I was trying to establish a skincare routine
I was into your whole entire deal
I was so ready to be endured

SHIP POEM

Do you think of the earth as alive or dead
I mean do you think we've killed it yet
It is the only thing we are good at
And we are so determined
I am like the president
I feel nothing for graves
My dreams are like a passenger ship
When I am standing on the shore
And they make that groaning sound
And the sea practically parts

SAILOR POEM

People look down on sailors
But this is a mistake
It makes so much sense
To look out at the ocean and vomit
Maybe you know someone unkind
Or someone worse than that
I know a lot of men
This is my third wave
Everyone in this boat is drunk
I will remember you like a horse
If I see you again I will tear my eyes out
And feel happy like a hill full of ants
It was great to have met you

ART FOR THE AFTERLIFE

ART POEM

I was invested in a life of destruction
I was sending a message to the abyss
It was like all of the birds screaming at the cold
It was like everyone thinking about death at the same time
I am feeling amiss
Supposedly due to how the planets are arranged
It is like a map of daffodils
Some words are coming out of my mouth
Like a planet nobody asked for
Wanting to figure into your astrology
It is like eating the same meal for sixteen years
It is like disappointing people through art

JURASSIC POEM

I will never be as good as Jurassic Park
Though I have put my entire life on screen
The truth hangs like a fart
Flowers are nice
Because they are a kind of skin you can tear apart
We are doing so crazy
We are already in the moon
I will put a flamingo on the cover
And watch it migrate around the room
And abandon myself to the movement

GRAPES POEM

I have a book of problems
It is a useless way to say things like
I love you and I am disappointed
And other things that are more complicated than that
Like is a dream a portent or a cause of grief
You were like a demon coming to my bed every night
Sitting on me like a sack of grapes
I was wanting your sweetness

LOVE POEM

I am secretly wonderful like a lost letter or a black pie
I am tired of being a lot
It is like cutting the arms off a tree
And you are left with knots
It is like knowing what everyone is thinking all the time
It is like being a woman
I would hate for you to write a long song about it
It would be like the end of a long vacation
It would be like a world without Courtney Love

ICE-CREAM POEM

We were as proud as mathematicians
We hated each other frivolously
I kept on wondering
Why everything had to be so stupid
I loved it when we used to say
I didn't ask for this
It was a kind of victory
Exactly the size and shape of an ice-cream dish

BIRD POEM

I have cried an entire bird for you
Still I would like to learn to speak French
And I would like a bird made from your crocodile tears
Some days I'll just be thinking of my own original bones
My arms seem sturdy like a rocking chair then
And it works perfectly
And it will last a long time
And I am amazed by the bird that stays

FLOWERING POEM

When I go to the flowering place
It is like a penis going limp inside me
And it is like wearing black the next day
And I need to see your face next to another face for context
And I could use a little help
When I go to the flowering place
You are either asleep or composing music
When you wake up you will think of me
But when you die you will think of something else

PARADE POEM

After a parade the earth is bored and covered in beads
As a woman I can relate
As a man I am looking for my right shoe
I am actually terrified of being this slow
Scream into my face or anything
Even the bad times seem good

TRAP POEM

I am very fragile but also resilient
Like some kind of flower that won't die
It is like someone forging on ahead without you
On the Oregon Trail
People aren't going to wait around forever
Watching you grope around in the dirt
My mind is a trap that laid itself
It can't be undone

LUCKY POEM

I was very lucky before I met you
The luckiest I ever was is when I was eight
The second most lucky is before I became alive
You are an impossible person
It is like watching someone walk around in the dark
I could actually cry
I don't think of you anymore
But I still send you flowers in my sleep

MOUNTAIN POEM

I was trying to impress you with poetry
Because I am an idiot
I wish I could say things like a river with an open mouth
Your body seems like an old-fashioned carriage
When I am herding you into a ditch
With a will like a mountain dog
That has been against me from the beginning
And it is a maniac
And it will not be tamed

DRUNK POEM

This is like when I am drunk after a party
This is like tipping over trashcans in the alleyway
It is such a power move
You kiss me when I am talking about my fear
And you kiss my bravery
My loneliness is like a bright star then
Far away and perilous and I am not ready

PARTY POEM

I did a good job inventing you
Or texting you or whatever it was
Getting you to put your tongue on my neck
When my thoughts hit the floor
It is like waving at the wilderness from coach
It is like saying the wrong thing at a party
And somebody hugs you goodbye

MOON UNIT

SUN POEM

I would like more time to look at the sun
The sun is totally without pretense
Shining its cancer onto everyone
I am finding corners of the house to sit in
In this corner I gaze at the sun and feel peaceful
I am so tired all the time
I wonder what I am saving money for
Life would be a great movie if it would end
And it will it will

MELON POEM

I would like to melon for you
And I would like to open obviously
And black seed
And garden grow
I would like to bask in the sun
And cum in the dirt
And get unstuck
When you are losing your phone before dawn
Unmelonlike to wander my love
I gaze at the moon

SAVED POEM

I have tapped into the river where poetry is always happening
And now poetry is always happening to me
It is like falling in love with a stranger
It is like accepting Jesus into your heart
Yes I am saved!

EMPIRE POEM

When I found you I was so surprised
It is like how I fell in love with the sky
It was like if God was saying
How about something you never thought of before
And how about if it is a whole empire
You were my favorite empire
You had a voice like when the sun is setting
You had this kind of way about you
You were the empire that was the greatest

PLANT POEM

This is like the sun waiting patiently
To receive anything at all
And a plant reaching towards it like an idiot
This is confusing art for virtue
And becoming the queen of the dump
And being quiet and falling

TRIUMPH POEM

In a poem I am as perfect as a robin's egg
In a poem I am triumphant yes
In a poem I say yes
In a poem I conquer death
And the battlefield is gorgeous
And the blood is vivid
And I am finally ready
When there is no one else around

BIRTHDAY POEM

This is a memory that is as loud as a waterfall
And it is a pretty dangerous waterfall
And you should actually be careful
This is like the perfect outfit for every occasion
It is like entering a flowering garden on your birthday
And we look really exceptional
And we feel like a thousand Floridas
And we could just die laughing in our birthday hats

ECLIPSE POEM

This is like a rambunctious lobotomy
This is like a total eclipse of the heart
I don't have any friends
I will buy everything in floral print to make up for it
It will be like when the sky is falling in waves
I keep trying to hurt you
But you are really just so tough
You have to just swallow you whole
Oh dear I just woke up

MOON POEM

Tonight the moon looks like a billboard for the moon
I am like an Academy Award
I am given to the best actor

TRAGIC POEM

I hate it when your bones shine through your skin
You seem unbearably mortal then
I start to wonder what is going on in your teeth
I think it is like a tragedy

BREAKFAST POEM

I am not interested in what you are saying
I would only like to be a sharp plant
I would like it to be a different time of day
When I stop thinking what I am thinking about
I eat disappointments like you for breakfast
I said to no one
I feed them but the plants won't talk

FEMININE POEM

It is a feeling better than soap
To hear you say a nice thing
Maybe you will text me from the inside of a flower
Let me drift into my drafts
It is a quiet girlish place
Like Eden feminine wash

SUN POEM

What a sky actually
Beyond it are the stars and the planets
It keeps going
I have decided to hate you for 100 days
As soon as I figure out the first day
After that you will become a figment
It will be very spiritual
I will cum in the corner looking at the sky
Thinking this is real this is love

FUTURE MOODS

END POEM

The world is ending and it seems like a good call
In my dream we were young again
Which can never happen again
And we were in love again
Which can never happen again
And we cared about each other
Like a couple of wild animals
It's too bad I had to lie and cheat to get to you
But I would have done much worse
And in fact I am pretty evil
The world is outrageously lonely
God is like a movie executive going shut it down
We could act a little more disappointed

EARTH POEM

You want to know the future
To humor you I try to sound it out
But I only make asshole sounds like Los Angeles
All day the earth is pulling us into itself
It is really relentless
One day we will get there
I am just like the earth
I want everything inside me
And I am big and ancient
Bigger and more ancient than everything else around
You have to be like that
If you want to absorb death
The earth will outlive us all
They should make movies about it

LAST POEM

The trees seem worth talking about today
We talk about the trees as a way to be not kissing
I don't want to lie
I am trying to think of something else
When we die
Everything from the earth will thank us
And grind up our bones up
As a last favor

CITY POEM

The city is like a photograph of a painting of a city
Some days it is not very hard
But sometimes it is like being part of a vast system
Where there is no one to talk to
The cat is licking its dick politely I guess
The rain barks like a scary dog
The moon has never seemed so full of itself
I understand this is a life of mediocrity
I have prepared in every possible way

COMMERCIAL POEM

You could learn everything there is to know
About this city from a commercial
That is why God is ready to flush it away
It is taking so long
I dream about the Midwest
And I will always dream about the Midwest
And I can see the romance in it
There are some things you can almost see
Like a love that goes moderately
Like a field loves corn

SURPRISE POEM

I asked how it was going
Out there in the desert
And you said I'm not there anymore
I thought I knew everything about you
But I guess I am an idiot

BOY POEM

Boys are very special
Girls you know
But boys
They're very special
Remember that time you cried
It was my favorite of the times
I wanted to protect you and you wanted to protect me too
It was so nice
I saw you going away
It seemed like a hole diminishing
You were going away and I was standing still
But there wasn't any difference

REPUBLICAN POEM

It is a little bit annoying
How every single person is a self-contained universe
And every person is a beetle that has just found its wings
Every single person can't imagine being a terrible person
No no no they can't
Even republicans
And I am so sorry
And I cannot tell if I mean it
I want to believe I'm making the future really terrible for everyone
And also the present

WHALE POEM

America you only speak the language of finance
But you are not so expensive
You are like a label with two wrong letters
You roll up like a rotting whale carcass with pinstripes
And I am amazed

MONEY POEM

Steal from corporations
My sister darlings
They are stealing our time
And it is all we have
We are worth so much more than money
But they are stealing our money too

ROOM POEM

You are on the other end of a computer
At the other end of the room
It feel you might attack at any moment
It is always better at the other end
At some point someone was about to be loving me
That would have been a good time to say wait
These thoughts are like beans and peas

PRETTY POEM

Life is like a room that is made up of other rooms
And being alive is like wanting to go outside
And loving someone is like making an opening into an unknown room
And being not in love is when the room starts to seem uninteresting
Or when the room closes off
When the world ends
It will be like all of the rooms falling out of place
It will be so pretty

CHAMPAGNE POEM

Everything was true and then it wasn't
It was like a miracle in reverse
It was like a very long goodbye
Everyone wanted it to be over and then it was over
It was a remarkable career in advertising

DOUBLE FANTASY

FANTASY POEM

You are like your own evil twin
It is like entering a world of dangerous flowers
It is like watching a wolf fight a fox
It is like a lazier double fantasy
I am made quite speechless
By the flowers and by spring
And by how one day the earth will just stop
It is an inordinate amount of feeling
It is like a suicide note that goes on too long
It is like crashing your own funeral
It should have been more like laying down
In a benevolent flower

DOG POEM

I am like a dog with a pearl in its teeth
It is a kind of precious thought
That bends but doesn't break
We are like two cities with different moons
There is no way to know the time
We are like two elephants at a dinner party
We must really learn to be more delightful
Sometimes I will just drive into a parking lot
I don't know where to be in this world
We are supposed to live and die at the same time
It must be like falling out of a jeep

LEMON POEM

I was glad when there was a story in your mouth
And it sounded like a long story with two graves
I hoped it would save me from all this poetry
I thought to smash my face into another face
And I thought it was very clever
I felt the bats in my belfry go noisome then
I felt there was a falcon in my cheek
I didn't want the phone to ring
It is such a sad alarm
It is like a little lemon in your eye
Cutie cutie cutie please be quiet
Turn me into a solid with the power of not talking
Also when you look at me I feel insolent
Yes yes yes everything is very beautiful
With an expiration date

KALEIDOSCOPE POEM

Please do not hold my hand
Unless you want to hold my hand forever
Also please remember what I said about not talking
It is so important that you do not talk
Never tell a man that he is powerful
Then he will start to know it
Then it will become a bruise
Then it will start to look like a kaleidoscope
Then it will mistake pain for pleasure
If that is what you want me to do

WOLF POEM

You have to be more cautious with beautiful things
Or anything that is wonderful
I was not made to be understood
I am walking out on a limb
It is like teetering on a high branch
I am going to act really greedy
While rising dramatically out of a puddle
It will be like being struck with unendurable melancholy
Right in the middle of washing the dog

GIRL POEM

Maybe I will run away
With the girl from my 20s
If she is not still batshit
I love a girl as I love blankets
And I will be here in the blankets
Away from all the other things
In case you need me

ZAP POEM

I will dream about a girl
And the way she says little bitch
And the kind of beer she drinks
And what she does with the label
And how she zapped me with a stun gun
Right in the tits

DRUG POEM

My heart is like a bomb
They say that you should not say bomb in a relationship
Also you should try not to have so many feelings
It is like that thing they say
About a rock and a freebase
I wanted you like drugs

COIN POEM

You are like a hill with no top that has been cut from the bottom
You are like one-sided coin
I love you but as a gift it is a weapon
Being as how you want to kill yourself
And everything that loves you
And everything that doesn't
It is the most intolerable kind of suffering
It is the kind that appears on the cover of TIME magazine
You act like a member of an upstanding committee
And I wish you would stop

CAKE POEM

It is not even interesting when you are cruel
It is like beating a fence when you could walk through
And it will take too long
And you will never find me
After a long time you will ask for a clue
And I will say ok and do nothing
You should have a cunt built into your forehead
I feel like Rapunzel making a cake
And I have heard of a widespread theory of death
Spin me around six times
And I will walk into a lonely grave

CROWN POEM

I thought I could make you like me again
It was like looking for a star someone described to me once
I am more like a lot of planets than a beautiful planet
You are like a song that won't stop
I could put the stars on your head
But you would think it was a nice crown for you to wear
And I mean no such thing

HORSES POEM

I am like a carrier pigeon when I am smiling
When I am eating your liver behind a glass door
You could crush me like a pile of horses
But you act like two squirrels fighting over a nut
And you are too difficult

KANSAS POEM

Every building seemed possible
And I was enjoying the performance of it
We were not as evil then
But thick as thieves and sick as dogs
I hadn't the slightest suspicion
The story of us is like the story of Kansas
It is like swallowing a fist
It is like when your sanity comes crawling back to you
In the middle of the night
And you hold it out again like a tooth

SOUR TIMES

SOUR POEM

My love it is starting to look like a pretty bad time
The future seems like an eternal shit
And sour like the mind of a pervert
I find you steady like a tent in a storm
I find you like you find a shell to cut your foot
I find you even though your skin has gone transparent
Like some kind of gross animal that washes up
To demonstrate how it might love you better than me
Let me cum while I describe to you the sunset
You can plainly see in front of you
And lay my head down on your soft genitals
And know that it is completely hopeless

PUNK POEM

I don't know is punk still a thing
I should leave the boys alone I think
Let them move to New York
It means something different now
It means they will build software
I tuck my shirt half in and wonder if it is right
Well it's too late now
I thought that boy was a trashcan I said and laughed
And looked around and noticed I was alone
There is nirvana but there is no one to talk to

CLOUD POEM

I am sorry I am like this
Remember how I said that all the time
You should have said it too
And you did you did
We were both so sorry
We kept looking at each other
Wondering what the other one would do
Love was a pink cloud we were standing in
It was a good excuse to walk off a cliff
Now I am as light as 10,000 magnolia blossoms
That is what you do in my memory
You and your fabulous fetishes
Which I miss sincerely

OVEN POEM

I guess I'm bent into the shape of you
Like a fender after a crash
I can only drag myself along wondering what you're thinking
I would like to wear a coat like a bruise
Campy shot of a calendar's pages flying off
Yeah it is too late to tell the truth
I am looking for a fine line
When I find it I will give myself a gold star into a lake
I will think of something I used to do
I will think a long thought
Some people can go outside whenever
And laugh and everything
I have to spare you the thought of me
That is why I have learned to fuck like a man

MEDULLA POEM

I was just sitting here when someone stole my umbrella
At least they're keeping dry I thought
I am not the subject of 300 sonnets
Because I have no grace
And because I am like the echo of a burgeoning chainsaw
And some kind of indistinguishable yellow crop
And also besides that
Love is just an occasion for poetry
And a reason for me to love you
When the air goes sour and sharp between us
I like for you to tell me how to feel
It is a childlike brutality
It is like holding a candle to the sun
You can study it in three million paintings of your long legs
And in my medulla oblongata
The place where you were born inside me before I was even born

DISNEY POEM

You put your mouth around my mouth like Disney
Think of all the spit we've shared
How can anything be called romantic
When you wipe your face on my leg
I love that vulgar gesture
We don't have to call it anything
The sun will come up
I will forget my underwear
Everything can be forgotten

GHOST POEM

You are like a ghost that has never even been alive
It is so exhausting having to explain everything to you
It is a violence against women
Like this endless stream of commercials on weight loss
You used to think my thoughts were so important
I used to tell them to you one at a time
I was just laying here in the road
You make me think of everything
Your misery is like a sport
You made me dance once and you made me laugh once
And I can't figure out how you did that

CALIFORNIA POEM

My face turned into a root
I would like to live
But most of the time I just don't exist
It is actually exhausting
My sadness is like an ex-lover
Starting a new life in a foreign country
With someone I have never met
In four years it will text me after the divorce
To say what's up I'm in California

CLOUD POEM

Should we apologize eleven more times into a cloud
It is like our insatiable need for parking lots
What is being razed to make room for all these apologies
The fields seem to exist
As natural as an argument between us
Remember the time you saw me and you stopped
And I was afraid of the stopping
And you said hi and I was afraid of it
And I was talking a little too loud

X-MAS POEM

Here comes the ghost of x-mas past
To fuck us up again
I am sending you letters without a return address
That only say hey how is it going
You are like Donald Duck with no pants
I like to watch you walk around in your white ass
I am feeling generous and treacherous
And straight up having a terrible time
And it is all for you Damien

HEART POEM

Here in the fireplace of my heart
Where good thoughts go to disappear
Here in the butthole of my chest
The sun comes up and I abandon myself
I have only a couple of teaspoons of care
And a darkness in my throat
You are so patient
It is almost enough to make me behave
I am in awe of a man with restraint
Who will leave quietly in the middle of the night

POOL POEM

No I have not yet found a way to be happy
With you still in the world
My bravery is sitting tight in a pool during a thunderstorm
Watching your reflection in the glass
My body is protecting me from death
It is exactly like nothing is happening
I have no time for miracles
Later I will roll you up and smoke you
And put your remainder in a bowl and smoke that too
And watch you hang around me like a very light fear
Making me know that everything is a lot
The worst thing you can think of is a pretty bad time
And I would like to rub your face in it

MARCH POEM

It is kind of beautiful in my cubicle dressed in black
Like almost as beautiful as a parking lot
Every little while I think about cum
You are careful like
When I leave the plants out on the patio to live or die
Someday I too will live or die
You kiss me like I have some answers in my mouth
I wonder when you will stop
I like to practice my goodbyes
Like a crowd of you is getting ready to join a march

INFINITE SADNESS

INFINITE POEM

I am so tired of this worship
You say you want peace but it is too ridiculous
Soon there can be a bomb for everything
A bomb for wolves
A bomb for holes
A bomb for anthills
A bomb for clovers
We won't be finished until it's done
It will be like an infinite sadness
It will be like a song we can play to ourselves
When we are ready to go to sleep

EGG POEM

Why can't I stop talking
I have to go on like a drip
I have to use water imagery because of my horoscope
I have to be alone all the time because of past lives shit
My aunt says I should work at McDonald's
Love is like a basket of eggs
And crushing each one
And every time thinking
What a beautiful foot
One thing you can know is that you are wrong about everything
And so is everyone

SANDBOX POEM

I would be the spirit of the corner lot
And I would even be the sandbox
On a Saturday morning
After wake n' bake
Smelling like piss
We can never go back Alexis
See how the clouds blow apart
That is exactly us

QUEST POEM

Saying anything at all is so dangerous
It is like lighting a match in a world with no wind
And you have to put the fire someplace
And where are you going to put the fire
And there is no place to put the fire
I want to be loud and driving with six quests
And someone to kiss my dick

FRUIT POEM

If I were a river I would drown you
And I would have you
The world is coming alive for this poem
But all I can think to say is that I love you
It is so embarrassing
Like only wanting to eat spoiled fruit

HAMLET POEM

You are like a hamlet
And you are like the prince of the basement
And you are like a cool place where I don't belong
My mother said it was like you always wanted something from me
I am running up against a wall
And I am so tired
You should be soft like I like you to
And lie down when you lie down
And be more like a lovely wall that I can lie down on

ROCKET POEM

You have a brain like a rocket ship
The point is only ever just to find a way out
I don't know what you mean ever
Are we right for each other
Define soon
Define right for each other
Define the best thing
These and lots of other words trouble me
When they are coming out of your mouth and otherwise
The only thing that should be in your mouth is me
I want so much to rub your jaw loose where it is tight
And to become very clear like a tendon

RIVER POEM

Aging is about so much more
Than your skin just changing
It's like watching your dreams fall into a river
I was you once I want to say
To everyone who won't look anymore
This is an admission of guilt
This is like failing to do any better

DATE POEM

I am like a blue suit
I don't know why there should be 30 of me going over a cliff
But I feel strangely proud like a glass full of glass
You have to be more cautious with beautiful things
Or anything that is wonderful
Perversion is the great inventor they say
Maybe if we took a long walk
We could engage with nature in a respectful way
Then we wouldn't have to be a gender
It can be so nice inside the grocery store
Standing in front of the dates
The color mauve can make it feel like the inside of a spaceship

COMET POEM

This is like a quiet emergency
This is like a comet making a phone call in space
Please do not argue
Between me and everything is something a little transparent
It's just something I noticed while being hurled through space
The earth is a busy place
And hot in the middle
I would gladly keep it in me like a plastic egg
There are several important things I neglected to tell you
Whatever I might say please believe
I am only ever thinking of my stomach

MATH POEM

I too speak in a perfect math
That doesn't make sense to anyone
I am a good egg
Countless among my brothers and sisters
I have traveled far with the brake on
Tie my hair in knots
These are the times we will want to forget
Very well
I am talking to you now about the cemetery
Where you lied down like an arrogant corpse
And I was so much more beautiful than a grave

BLANK POEM

It is beautiful when we don't meet
I get happy walking around inside me
Too old to be driving around without insurance
There was something like an urgent blank
I hope I die with my face up
Looking at the stars
Ninety miles outside the city
Where the darkness shines its own kind of light
I am trying to lay it out like gossamer

BEAUTIFUL POEM

You would like me to keep looking at you the way I do
And like ok
If it will keep you around
It is like pogs or marbles
Little pieces of yourself
For little pieces of somebody else
I want you like a hot iron down the spine
You say I think it's beautiful and sad
And you are right and thank you
Thank you very much

With thanks to:

Mallory for her support over the years

Taylor
Mik
Chris Rovee
Lara
Chris Barrett
Janet
Chioke

And to the journals in which these poems appeared:

Hobart
House Party Poetry
HTML Giant
Maudlin House
Neutral Spaces
Peach Magazine
WaxNine

Laura Theobald is a PhD student in English at UGA in Athens. She's the author of three books of poetry: *Salad Days* (Maudlin House, 2021), *Kokomo* (Disorder Press, 2019), and *What My Hair Says About You* (Metatron Press, 2017), and three chapbooks. She received an MFA from LSU, where she served as the editor of the *New Delta Review*, and continues to design books for small press publishers. Her poetry has appeared in *jubilat, The Volta, Peach Mag, The Atlas Review, Everyday Genius*, and *Black Warrior Review*, among others, and in the anthology *Women of Resistance*. Her criticism has appeared on *The Harriet Blog*. She's on Twitter and Insta as lidleida.

I will put a flamingo on the cover

And watch it migrate around the room

And abandon myself to the movement

www.ingramcontent.com/pod-product-compliance
Lightning Source LLC
Chambersburg PA
CBHW072010210726
48294CB00013B/1917